BRICK WALL

TRAFFIC CONE

.7

SIDE VIEW

8.2

1.1

1.2

.3

WHEEL BARROW

.5

.3

PICKAX

HARD...

HAT

SHOVEL

.3

.8

4.3

4.1

1.1

REAR VIEW

14.5

LATTICE

DAISY

For Matt.
Because he can lift the heavy stuff.

THIS IS A BORZOI BOOK PUBLISHED BY ALFRED A. KNOPF

Copyright © 2009 by Brie Spangler

All rights reserved. Published in the United States by Alfred A. Knopf, an imprint of Random House Children's Books,
a division of Random House, Inc., New York.

Knopf, Borzoi Books, and the colophon are registered trademarks of Random House, Inc.

Visit us on the Web! www.randomhouse.com/kids

Educators and librarians, for a variety of teaching tools, visit us at www.randomhouse.com/teachers

Library of Congress Cataloging-in-Publication Data
Spangler, Brie.
The grumpy dump truck / Brie Spangler. — 1st ed.
p.   cm.
Summary: Bertrand the dump truck is always grumpy and mean, but a chance encounter with a porcupine reveals that his bad mood has a cause.
ISBN 978-0-375-85839-0 (trade) — ISBN 978-0-375-95839-7 (lib. bdg.)
[1. Mood (Psychology)—Fiction. 2. Dump trucks—Fiction. 3. Porcupines—Fiction. 4. Construction equipment—Fiction.] I. Title.
PZ7.S7365Gru 2009
[E]—dc22
2008024528

The illustrations in this book were created digitally.

MANUFACTURED IN MALAYSIA
July 2009
10 9 8 7 6 5 4 3 2 1
First Edition

Once there was a dump truck.

And while he was good at his job . . .

. . . his attitude was rather

He was rude to the backhoe.

And he was a real pain to the crane.

He shouted at the foreman.

And he honked at the bricklayers.

. . . he ran into a problem.

Bertrand was furious.

Tilly tried to explain herself . . .

. . . **but Bertrand was still upset.**

Tilly tried again . . .

. . . but Bertrand wasn't convinced.

Tilly climbed up on a cinder block . . .

. . . and gently plucked out the quill.

But to her surprise, she found more than a quill in Bertrand's tire.

Tilly found a . . .

Suddenly Bertrand felt much better.

And for the first time, he said,

Bertrand wasn't so grumpy anymore.

SHOVEL

.3

PICKAX

.3

.5

TROWEL

LAND STA...

Red
Woo
Approx

14.5

LATTICE

CRANE

.9

CH

SIDE VIEW

8.2

1.1

TRAFFIC CONE

WALL

14.3